Not This Time ®

I0551317

Written by iRiS

Moore
Las Vegas
Nevada **P**ublishing

Not This Time

First Edition

Publisher's Note
This is a work of fiction with the use of Biblical text. Not intended to fictionalize Biblical references. All characters in this book are fictitious and any resemblance to real persons, living or dead is coincidental.

All biblical text is from the King James Version (KJV) or New King James Version (NKJV) unless otherwise noted.

Dr. Maya Angelou words of wisdom are from her status updates on Facebook.

Cover design and artwork by:
Madd House Illustrators & Design
Las Vegas, NV
Maddhouseillustrators@yahoo.com

Published by Moore Publishing a division of The Sumpter Group
3635 S. Fort Apache Road Suite 200-427 Las Vegas, NV 89147

Printed in the United States of America
ISBN- **978-0615489117**

Not This Time

Also by iRiS

Moving Forward in the Face of Adversity

It's Not You , It's Me!

It's Not You, It's Me – The Anthology

(A Book of Poems)

You Again?...

Not This Time

I dedicate this work to my
Mother Ollie Marie and
my Father Wilton Joseph Brown,
they departed this life prematurely:
Gave their love unconditionally!
I hope I live up to your Dreams for me to be the best me
I can be!

Not This Time

Table of Contents

Not This Time

Not This Time

The Journey

Not This Time

MAD AS HELL

I am mad as hell! If you are already offended this book is probably not for you. I started writing this book before the passing of my mother and before the release of You Again.

Yes, I love God, the fact remains I am mad, upset, perturbed and frustrated. In no way am I going to turn my back on all that I know and believe but, I am mad! I am mad that my mother is not here anymore. I am mad that my father is not here either. I am mad that I am living from penny to penny. True, all of my needs get met and God is faithful! But nothing has turned out the way I anticipated. There was a time when money and/or the access of money were at my fingertips, yet, today it feels like I am repelling abundance. Also, I am—*well, I am not telling my age*—tired of feeling aches and pains that should be for someone much older than I am. When I turn on the television I get disgusted at all the paid programming on TV, that make too good to be true promises: *"Your wish is Your Command;" "Put on your make-up like the stars:" "Clear Skin in 14 days;" "Lose*

2 sizes instantly;" "21 day Consciousness Cleans;" "Your baby can read;" "Can't sleep at night? Or don't want to wake up in the morning we promise help for both for only $19.95!"

I am JUST MAD!

I am sure *"they"* or *"some"* would say, *"You have much to be thankful for, someone would love to be in your shoes."* I know. I did not say I am not grateful or I do not appreciate my life, nevertheless I'm just mad!

The Church People, as my son calls them, are another set of irritations. For some *church people*, you cannot do enough, for others you do too much. We pray too loud, too long, not long enough, not enough teaching, too much teaching, we need more preaching, less preaching, more fellowships, too many fellowships, asking too much, maybe you should ask for more. I don't trust you, I put all my trust in you, pay my cell bill, get my nails done, you did not say that right or you were too nice. Then there is the other group of *church people* that says, I turned around 7-times, fasted 21 days, read a scripture a day, and gave a special seed offering and this stuff is not working! My life is a mess because the church, the preacher, the elder, or whomever doesn't understand. It's exhausting and enough to make you want to halla!

Angry, furious, livid, irate, infuriated, fuming annoyed, up in arms and beside myself! I said it! You want to say it, but in an effort to be spiritually correct, you are unwilling to! I am Mad!

Well I said it! I am MAD! Hot about it!

Disgusted that I made the choice to marry a numbskull who has not and is not capable of loving himself let alone his child or me; what *freakin'*, *flappin'*, *flippin'* problem I was having that once again I made an active choice to ignore the obvious. I had learned embraced, walked-a-way from mediocrity and was walking my Divine Purpose!

I do not know if I like this compulsive obsession pulling me without much effort into the incessant beat of purpose. Sometimes, I wonder if we are all demented walking head first into a ditch of influenced ignorance; because the pain of facing *reality* is just too much to bear. Not only that, I have gotten myself in a place where the weight of the world often feels as if it is on my shoulders, and all universal calamity is being carried and birthed through me.

I know that it is absurd, ludicrous, wacky, misguided, illogical, crazy and even foolish to think I and I alone carry the weight of the world and that all universal calamities are being carried and birthed through me. Or is it? I am the daughter of Abraham, an heir to the Kingdom, my Daddy owns *everything* and there is absolutely no reason I should be in need, want or desire for anything that will not only help me but those with whom I come in contact.

Now, if you are okay with living a mediocre life and calling it a sacrifice for the *kingdom*, that's you! However, I know that scripture says my sacrifice is my *life* and in giving my life and living, walking and abiding in Him *everything* else would be added to me. Anything short of that is not acceptable.

This journey of life is full of challenges, laughter, disappointment, joy and happiness. The thing I have come to terms with is, above all else, life is cyclical, circulatory. We either get in step with the cycle or create blocks that cause repetitive breakdowns in the constant flow of peace, joy and harmony.

Read with an open mind and heart! Let the words spill from the pages into your world and open you to the possibility and probability that it does not have to be that way, *Not this time!*

I promise, you will think, you may even see yourself on the pages, laugh and cry. And when it is all over you will say, *Not this time!*

Not This Time

MARRIED NOW

∞

"And the Angel of the Lord said to her, 'Behold you are with child and you shall bear a son. You shall call his name Ishmael, because the Lord has heard your affliction. He shall be a wild man; His hand shall be against every man, and every man's hand against his. And he shall dwell in the presence of all his brethren."

Genesis 16:11-12

∞

Hagar became intertwined with someone else's destiny while having a destiny of her own. There was a distinct fulfillment and lesson for Hagar, through her relationship with Abraham and Sarah. Their lives became interconnected due to process and destiny!

What Hagar did not know was that the impatience of Sara and Abram would push her into an encounter with

God that would cause her to give birth to His revelation for *all* to see throughout generations.

∞

F athers Day 2008 I sat in service and listened to a very powerful message. A family and its children need their father. Only so much a mother can do and teach, but the impact of a man and or father makes a difference in a male and female child.

"Married with no father in the house; my marriage is now Ishmael. Is it because I, along with millions of others, have learned to find scriptures to validate what we want to do? Or is it a true revelation of what God has said and is saying about life and destiny? Heaviness was looming over my head. A stroke of somberness filled my soul and yet I had a desire to be with him. Bruised but not broken, my heart is still open; Joss Stone was the melody on the airwaves.

∞

"And I say to you, whoever divorces his wife, except for sexual immorality and marries another commits adultery and whoever marries her who is divorced commits adultery (10) His disciples said to Him if such is the case of the with is wife, it is better not to marry."

Matthew 19: 9-10

"But I say to the unmarried and to the widows. It is good for them if they remain even as I am (9) but if they cannot exercise self control let them marry. For it is better to marry than to burn with passion."

1Corinthians 7: 8-9

∞

This time I finally got it right I was pregnant and married. It didn't matter that the man I married—*Mr. who in the world are you?* —seven months earlier had a serious problem. I had no idea how serious. I thought his words, *I am clean and I will never use again meant something.* His words did mean something: —*I should have run for the border.*

Instead the proposal of marriage was an obvious solution to a very common problem. Packaged differently and obviously after being on the path of a very fulfilling life, I had mastered my fears and put the past where it belonged, behind me. In a successful career with a fortune 500 companies, completed my first major book. Purchased my first home, actively living and experiencing the word of God, my non-profit business was growing, so why in the world would a relationship at this point be dangerous?

The usual just friends, in fact I had no desire or inclination to see him as more than a friend. I enjoyed his company, but kept my distance. You know that very potent stimuli *conversation:* nonthreatening, open, uninhibited talk. No harm, *right*! Wrong. It was just like the serpent that appeared to Eve, *You will not surely die….*Well, after a one year friendship and a trip to Las Vegas we got married. There was nothing wrong with that. The marriage bed is undefiled, right?!

How, could I position myself to get so far off track and out of purpose? What I did was ordained by God, marriage isn't wrong. It is sanctioned. My very essence and divine destiny was smothered by the prospect of helping this man. Fulfilling my destiny in him, with him; energy leaked from the portals of my veins, as if a nurse had inserted a butterfly needle to withdraw blood to save the life of another human being.

The enjoyment and ecstasy of marriage was short-lived after an extremely uneventful ceremony at the Justice of the Peace. Never married, had no children, making over six figures, and was spiritually stable—so I thought. I married a man with *nothing* but the words: *I love you! I want to be with you the rest of my life! And I will never use again! You have made the difference in my world.*

Two weeks after this monumental occasion I returned home to find an intoxicated shell staring into a world of an uncommon cycle of destruction. The honeymoon was over, before it started. Not rehabs, meetings, tears, counseling, nor *I am having a baby* changed the fact I was connected to a cocaine addicted man who could not, would not; neither had it in him to stop! I was married to a crack-head!

The very joy of a relationship mirroring what I talked about was all up in smoke literally and there was nothing I could do about it. Ishmael was born and Isaac was on the way. I questioned if I knew God, I wondered if my own deliverance from insane living was legit. What I thought I was clear through revelation and experience were distant, clouded with a pipe dream and now becoming a fleeting memory. God's fulfilled security in my life was a lingering unfulfilled fantasy and I was trapped in a web of deceit and make believe promises. I was married to a man who not only had an addiction which stemmed from a spiritual malady he was unable to deal with it. My soul was now mish-mashed like mashed potatoes to his confusion. A relationship out of season was birthed. God was obviously not done with me and apparently I had not yet learned the lesson of staying focused.

∞

"Now Sarai, Abrams wife, had borne him no children: And she had an Egyptian maidservant whose name was Hagar. So Sarai said to Ab-ram, "See now the Lord has restrained me from bearing children. Please go in to my maid; per-haps I shall obtain children by her." And Abram heeded the voice of Sarai."

Genesis 16:1-2

∞

Abram didn't do anything against Sarai. She gave him permission to be with Hagar and attempt to get Hagar pregnant. Sarai's motive was Hagar could give Abram a son and they would still be in legal rights. They would not be breaking a so-called covenant with their promise. It didn't appear to be an apparent problem since it was legal to do what they did right?

∞

Fights, leaving me stranded in my car, money missing, him staying away for weeks at a time, and me, Iris, too embarrassed to tell anyone what was going on. Early one Tuesday in June 2004 I woke up! Not just got out of bed but woke up out of a deep sleep. I looked around our condo and realized, if anyone were to walk in this place right now…they would think I was a crack head. Scheduled for a biopsy, my doctor recommended that I take another pregnancy test, just to make sure I was not pregnant.

Alright, I am sure, I am not pregnant.

An hour later the blood work returned POSITIVE; *Iris you are pregnant.* I wailed, tears running down my cheeks— not of relief, but I shuddered while thinking of his blood coursing through me. My doctor, of course, was not expecting such a response.

Well Mrs. Who in the World are you? you are not happy about this?

Nooooooooooooo! I wailed.

He handed me tissue. *Well what is the problem? You are married, I am sure your husband will be happy.*

Oh nooooooo, he, he nooooooo, I released rivers of sadness again. Attempting to compose myself he proceeded

O.k. I see the Dr. said. Well I do not have the answers for you, but the following are your options.

I was a very high-risk pregnancy. I could terminate, but I would have to make a quick decision. I left the doctor's office only to return to the place I once called home, where my husband had taken the last few items for another hit!

A fur coat, jewelry, CD player and whatever else I did not notice at the time. Furious, is an understatement. My state of mind was not clear at all. I am sure if I had a baseball bat and he was anywhere near me I would have bashed his head in a few times, as if that would knock some sense into him. Probably not; he would just get up, find his pipe and start smoking—so sad.

My love for him could not and would not cure him. My patience and understanding would not save him. I was at a crossroad, Ishmael or Isaac. Although my thoughts wanted to render a verdict it's not me, it's him. I knew the search inside was inevitable.

Contemplating what to do, I thought about the night I probably got pregnant. They say a wife cannot be raped. But if you do not want to have sex, say no and your husband forces him self on you and in you what is that? After another crack binge we were in the car and he was driving like a manic.

Please slow down. I pleaded.

He was acting like a bull dog. I had experienced this intimidating spirit before. I do not think it was influenced by drugs, but the spirit behind the action of intimidation I had encountered before with Mr.

everything I hoped for. The culprit once again I wouldn't concede a request. This time money, he wanted me to give him money and he wanted to take the car. I said no. Running red lights talking erratically, I begin yelling...

Stop the dang car!

Attempting to take control of the steering wheel –as if I could stop this 230 plus pound man— but by this point I was insane. He moved his arm and hit me in my jaw.

See! See what you made me do woman...Oh God!

I cried.

Just take me home! Take me home!

Furious, I knew the only way I was going to get away from him was to make him think I would not leave him. I could hear my mother *when you are in the Lions mouth you have to ease your head out slowly; otherwise you might get your head yanked off.*

We got in the house, him apologizing...grabbing at me, kissing me, telling me I was not going to leave him, I would forever be connected to him. Silent, starring into his eyes he threw me on the bed. Ripping my clothes off;

Stop Mr. who in the world are you?

No I do not want to!

Oh yes, I am going to put a baby inside of you and you are never going to leave me.

Numb! Lifeless! I laid. He finished his business turned over and fell asleep.

Unable to move, Niagara Falls gushes out of my eyes.

Oh God, what have I gotten myself into?

∞

A powerful lesson had to be learned. The lesson of knowing the difference between what is legal and what did God say about your decision. I could not afford to be clear as mud. Crystal clear decisions had to be made. If the road I was on did not reflect my *Dream or Vision* it was time to make a U-turn. It was me again, but I was sure a repeating cycle was not the choice, *Not This Time*.

∞

Legal does not mean it is spiritually sound or appropriate for the course of your life. The feelings of being by myself doing it by myself, missing the window of opportunity had pushed me in a standoff with Destiny verses Legal. Clear on what God had shown me through my desires and inspiration; however, what I was engaged in didn't reflect that picture. The burden and pain of those who did not understand or wished to give me their advice, advice that did not reflect the word revealed to me, forced me to the doorstep of fulfillment & possibly not experiencing fulfillment. I could not bear living in this world with only a tease, glimpse or taste and not having the whole kit and caboodle.

∞

Moses did not make it to the Promise land because he did not follow the instructions of God. God said, *Speak to the rock* and the water will spring forth.

"Take the rod, and gather thou the assembly together, thou, and Aaron, thy brother, and speak ye unto the rock before their eyes; and it shall give forth its water/life, and thou shall bring forth to them water out of the rock; so thou shall give the congregation and their beasts drink."

Numbers 20:8

These were very specific instructions. God included who to take with him, how to handle the difficult hard place and said in doing this I will provide water to drink representing an abundant life. Why was this so significant? Especially, since this was after the miracle of the parting of the Red Sea.

Scripture says because their obedience, which represented belief in Him; following the instruction to the letter, would *sanctify* Him, or bless, consecrate, make holy, make sacred, purify and approve Him in the eyes of the Children of Israel.

"And Moses lifted up his hand, and with the rod he smote (hit) the rock twice; and the water came out abundantly, and the congregation drank and their beast.

And the Lord spoke to Moses and Aaron, because ye believed me not, to sanctify me in the eyes of the children of Israel, therefore ye shall not bring this congregation into the land which I have given them."

Numbers 20:11-12

What Moses and Aaron did was *legal* and it produced the desired result water for the people to drink. However, it did not fulfill the purpose, which was to *sanctify* the Lord in the eyes of the people. So instead of sanctification being born it gave birth to *strife*.

This is the water/life of Mer'ibah, (strife)

Numbers 20:13

The children of Israel drank from the water of *strife or the life of strife. Strife is the bitter sometimes violent conflict or dissension: an act of contention: exertion or contention for superiority;* and still the children of Israel strove, *(to devote serious effort or energy: endeavor: to struggle in opposition)* with the Lord for God to be sanctified in them meaning for the Gods blessings, abundance or to be approved by God.

Abram followed the same pattern of dis-obedience. He had specific instruction that Sarai would give him a son, but he allowed Sarai to convince him to lay with her handmaid. It was legal (of the flesh) because she gave permission, but it was not apart of their promise.

A son was born, Ishmael; and the son was blessed. Because he was born outside of the promise strife was also given birth as well. Oh My God! At some point and time we have all walked in unbelief, which is disobedience to the revelation of God as it relates to our divine purpose and destiny. I could see how my choice had given birth to strife.

∞

Identifying patterns, the processes and protocols of those gone before us gives opportunity for each of us to move beyond a wrong turn, bad choice, and decision. The clear choices may not be a *sin*, but one wrong choice can alter the course of your life. One choice can place you on a cycle of unnecessary weight and responsibilities.

Paul says, *I have a thorn in my flesh to remind me constantly of some of the choices I have made. But praise God I use this thorn for His glory. I can never forget that it is only because of God's grace that I am walking in purpose and fulfilling the promises He has given me.*

And lest I should be exalted above measure through abundance of the revelations, there was given to me a thorn in the flesh, the messenger of Satan to buffet me, lest I should be exalted above measure. For this thing I besought the Lord thrice (three times) that it might depart from me. And he said unto to me My grace is sufficient for thee, for my strength is made perfect in weakness, Most gladly, therefore, will I rather glory in my infirmities (consequences of my choices) that the power of Christ may rest upon me. Therefore I take pleasure (resolve) in infirmities, in reproaches, in necessities, in persecution for Christ's sake, for when I am weak, it is then I am strong.

2 Corinthians 12:7-10

∞

Oh God Please! Help me relinquish what I think I know about this life, myself, my family and especially You so that I may have an open mind and a fresh experience with this life, myself, my family and especially You God. A familiar space yet different.

Are you ready to live a life you never lived and create a world that does not exist? What made me ask this man this question?

Mr. who in the world are you? Looked at me like a man in love. Yearning for what he had not yet tasted. Me! The essence of wisdom, knowledge understanding and prosperity, my nectar had not yet been experienced in its current state. Ripe, fresh and full of flavor and he sensed that.

Call it magnetism, pheromones, timing or a combination of all three. The question I ask myself sometimes to this day is what made me ask this man this question? After spending an afternoon together we laughed and shared strong attraction. Our friendship was taking a turn I was not sure I wanted. He leaned in the car and gently swiped my lips with a kiss.

You are the life I never lived and world that has not yet existed...

...I jumped! Leaned back! I was not expecting the chemistry to be so electrifying. He smiled,

Call me when you get home.

∞

I awakened with this prayer on my lips. Last night I fell asleep with this prayer on my lips. Some would call my next experience a coincidence. I say it was divine providence.

In the midst of all difficulties and uncertainties, a simple intimacy had come into being for me: I had met myself, and found myself worthy. I had become beloved to myself. I discovered a whole new relationship with God and life. I contemplated my changing life, I actually felt a longing for a future time in which I might once again come to experience the magnificence of my own solitude; and, come again to know directly that wellspring of inner dignity and wholeness, which was filling in me and was now to flow through me into my life in the world outside.

I found intimacy with myself, intimacy and closeness with others when I gave up my need to be *right*. My search for a domestic partnership, revealed a whole new experience of sexuality as a non-addictive medium for me. I experienced a state of being acceptance of God and how God chooses to show up in life.

The brief stretch of bliss quickly demoralized into constant tension, worry, friction and rivalry with a nonhuman entity. Crack cocaine is not a force to be reckoned with. No womanly intuition or persuasion can out-think, out-seduce, or out-spend a relationship with Ms. Crack. If your mate has had an affair or is in an affair with her trust me, she is nothing to compete with; she is out of all mortal leagues. I would rather deal with a man having an affair with video games and outside flings with internet women than her.

In spite of brief outbursts of wanting to leave his long standing relationship with Ms. Crack and experience the real world, he had not yet realized his weakness, subjection, and craving to fulfill his insatiable desire. In the war of Iris verses Ms. Crack, Ms C always won!

Eventually, the contemplation of unconditionally loving him or me surfaced and I had to make a decision. Determination of what outweighed my quest for fulfillment was not only of paramount importance but was the only choice to determine how I would live the remainder of my life.

Was it my false hope of waiting for Mr. Right, having his baby or was it the acceptance of the now lesson? The lesson of being authentic in relationships with others— free to let go of self-serving power and prestige—as a driving motive to fulfill destiny. My career, which I used to define my success, exploited me for material security. Constantly it eluded me at the expense of my peace of mind; the dream of an American Dream Family was obviously a fleeting notion. Of course for most full blooded Americans this had become a lackluster dream, without debate, now a dream turned nightmare for me.

The mirror reflected me again and my selfish reasons no longer appealed to me. My usefulness as a channel for healing was a direct result of my experience in sick behavior, as well as in the healing of my unproductive habits. Medical terminology for this behavior is *co-dependency.*

∞

A psychological condition or a relationship in which a person is controlled or manipulated by another who is affected with a pathological condition (as an addiction to alcohol or heroin); *broadly*: dependence on the needs of or control by another.

Merriam Webster Dictionary

∞

My oh my! What a definition. I discovered I can continue to affirm healing by sharing with others. The source of love, which is of God, would flow from within me and had never left me. I alone had turned my back on what produced peace, serenity and harmony in my life…Hoping that I would not have to do this or be disciplined the rest of my life; hoping that I would not have to *be*. Hoping I would not have to acknowledge and accept that which I cannot change. I have found there is no other cure for my sick behavior, which opens the door to destructive living; the pendulum of nothingness painted imaginary pictures of empty hope and promises.

Healing has to be my life. Healing is my sharing, giving and loving without expectation or prediction to the outcome. Healing is being and living in the world of unconditional forgiveness which is love. Healing is seeking truth through My God and accepting how He shows up in my life. Embracing these truths—I have found serenity, wholeness and completeness. Healing is not being a doormat by the doorway to self discovery using false humility and obedience to God as an excuse for not acting upon truth not just facts. I am healing! The doorway to freedom! –A freedom in a hope and promise not given by mortal man.

I accept perfection in an imperfect world: the world of me. Love, mercy and grace are my healing tools which I choose to call My God.

Abraham pleased God because of His Faith Action....He moved in the direction of God...David was a man after Gods on heart because He worshipped Him-Action

Mr. who in the world are you? attempted to be apart of a world he was not yet ready for. I suppose he honestly gave an effort in creating a lifestyle he had not tasted. Unfortunately, his relationship with Ms. Crack outperformed, outlasted and pulled him into the familiar; for me this was a world I had no desire to be apart of; a tad bit too dark for my taste or liking. It took almost five years to accept, embrace and let go, of a dream that was not mine so that I could live in my world full of dreams and possibility.

WHEN IT IS BLOOD

I carried Isaac for nine months. In the face of knowing Ishmael was born too and there was nothing I could do about this fact. He was my husband. He was the father of my child. His blood was carousing through my body. Yet, a difficult choice was inevitable!

Another round of rehab! In an attempt to continue in the charade of *he is it!*

I wish I could stop; the truth is I do not want too! If I could only face that fact!

I think if he said those words I would at least have a little more respect for the man. Only because he had no other place to go and someone was out to kill him, did he return to rehab in my fourth month of pregnancy. Not to mention the superb medical coverage I had which covered one of the best rehabilitation centers in Southern California. I remember thinking,

"I cannot do this again!" "I cannot sit in another meeting and listen to the same reasons!"

He would say *I finally understand what the word – retarded— means. Someone said to me I was retarded and I would think.*

No, I am not. Because when you think retarded, you think of someone walking down the street with a limp and drooling at the mouth! But by definition the word retarded means; someone with the inability to think straight or make rational decisions.

Blah! Blah! Blah!—Yimmie Yang! Yimmie You!— I had heard this story at least a dozen times the words or definitions coming out of his mouth meant nothing. Empty and meaningless the scripture calls non-substance words tinkling cymbals and sounding brass. They had no power or sincerity. It sounded as hallow as his retarded brain! Very annoying! But this was my husband, the man I married. The man I choose to be the father of my child. This was a fact. It did not matter if I liked my choice neither did it matter I wished I never married him or made love to him. It didn't matter I wished the first time he messed up I left his stupid asinine butt alone forever; the bottom line—I now had an irrevocable soul connection. A child was in the picture. A blood covenant had been made and there was nothing to do, but accept.

∞

Although it is the law it may not be the grace. Marriage is honorable and will be honored by God because it is His law. Will grace cover it? Ishmael was not the promise God gave to Abraham. Because Sarah gave him the green light to have Hagar, the consummation was made legal. Abraham also prayed that the blessings be with Ishmael. However, it was not what God promised. He promised that Sarah would give birth to a son for Abraham. Did that mean Ishmael was not Abraham son? Did this mean Hagar was not the mother of his firstborn? Did it mean that Ishmael did not play a significant role in Abraham fulfilling Destiny?

∞

"And as for Ishmael, I have heard thee; behold, I have blessed him, and will make him fruitful, and will multiply him exceedingly; twelve princes shall he beget, and I will make him a great nation. But my covenant I shall establish with Isaac, whom Sarah shall bear unto thee at the set time in the next year."

Genesis 17:20-21

∞

All of my children where born; my child of destiny, my natural child and my husband. I knew God promised me a husband. He promised me a boy child. He also promised that I would fulfill the destiny of ministering, teaching and writing in such a candid, practical way that many would be healed from childhood wounds, emotional trauma as well as embedded scar tissue from unauthorized relationships.

So, how do I continue with Ishmael?

Ishmael was the product of impatience and doubt; nothing less or more than unbelief. Did this mean I could not now walk in my promise?

Would I have to live with this wrong turn for the rest of my life?

Was there a way to cut the ties although there is a blood connection?

∞

The result for the actions of Abraham and Sarah was the birth of Ishmael, and he was now his first born. God did not stop speaking to him and giving instruction on how to proceed in the face of creating an unauthorized, although *legal* situation.

They both received a name change after Ishmael was born. But Abraham had to hear the voice of God, know that the voice was God and then follow His instructions.

"And when Abram was ninety years old and nine (99), the Lord appeared to Abram and said unto him I am the Almighty God; walk before me, and be thou perfect.

And I will make my covenant between me and the, and will multiply thee exceedingly. And Abram fell on his face: and God talked with him, saying ..."

Genesis 17:1-3

∞

Why is this important?

In the face of chaos, inappropriate actions, the creation of situations that cannot be made to go away through prayer or fasting, you have to be able to still yourself before the living God and know when He is calling you!

Repentance is not only appropriate but it allows your hearing to become sensitive to the palpations of the Spirit within you.

You can hear Him say I will never leave you or forsake you!

My yoke is easy and my burden is light!

I order your steps! And in the midst of your mess I will get the glory.

All of this reassurance comes in stillness. Allowing the mind to quiet self—ceasing the chatter of trying to fix it, change it and alter the outcome. — It is in stillness you hear,

I can do all things through Christ that strengthens me.

This is not unto death, but for my glory!

In stillness direction and clarity reveals self.

∞

"As for me, behold, my covenant is with thee, and thou shall be a father of many nations. Neither shall thy name any more be called Abram, but thy name shall be Abraham; for a father of many nations have I made thee. And I will make thee exceedingly fruitful, and I will make nations of thee and kings shall come out of thee. And I will establish My covenant between Me and thee and thy seed after thee in their generations for an everlasting covenant, to be a God unto thee, and to thy seed after thee. And I will give thee, the land wherein thy seed after thee, the land wherein thou art a sojourner (stranger), all the land of Canaan, for an everlasting possession and I will be their God"

Genesis 17:4-8

∞

Abraham received this in stillness. Remember he fell on his face in the third verse, which was an act of reverence and stillness. However, he didn't get up from his face the place of reverence; he remained in reverence and stillness. Abraham had to get further instructions on how to receive the promise.

∞

"And God said to Abraham thou shall keep my covenant therefore, thou seed (children) after thee in their generation. This is My covenant, which ye shall keep between me and you and thy seed after thee: Every male child among you shall be circumcised. And ye shall circumcise the flesh of your foreskin; and it shall be a sign of the covenant between me and you. And eight days old shall be circumcised among you, every male child in

*your generations, he that is born in the house, or bought
with money of any foreigner who is not of thy seed. He
that is born in thy house, and he that is bought with
money, must be circumcised; and my covenant shall be
in your flesh for an everlasting covenant And the
uncircumcised male child whose flesh of his foreskin is
not circumcised, that soul shall be cut off from his
people; he hath broken my covenant"*

Genesis 17:9-14

∞

Again, specific instructions were given to Abraham:

Abraham sent Hagar and Ishmael away.

How could he send away his first-born? I am sure he
loved the boy and had feelings for his first-born.

Oftentimes, stillness doesn't quiet the mind from trying
to come up with alternatives and solutions to ease the
discomfort of the inevitable. However, it is only in
stillness that the Spirit can be heard.

My thinking ran marathons to figure out an easy or not
so confrontational way to deal with the chaos I had
created. *I have tried it all. I thought, prayed gave tithes,
been responsible, used wisdom, and avoided the pitfalls
of the same mistake.*

My dream of a fulfilled life only revealed the turmoil of
Spirit and Soul/Mind, to say I must stay focused so that I
do not miss this season. Another 10-year cycle of

acceptance and coming to terms is definitely not an option. I do not have that kind of time any more. I am older with a child now. I forge forward in faith and commitment—reminding myself of the tablets imprinted on my heart from the dreams transferred to me as a child. I encourage those around me, I give of my time, money, skills and talents only to find out I am still walking in the deep water and there is no shore on the horizon.

What I thought I saw or see is only the cycle of another trial and test.

When will this be over?

I taste a better life and get a glimpse of being debt and care free only to awaken up to another day that reminds me of Monday morning blues.

∞

Exhausted yet my senses are aroused to the nonconformity of agreement. My action revealed a confirmed lack of the indwelling Spirit that saturates a room and spills out victory and deliverance. Complaining of not enough love, everyone appearing not to have enough money; repeated struggles of providing an adequate roof only to meet another man that does not have his stuff together: *Mr. I don't think so.* His conversation or illusion is not strong enough to pull me away this time. The mere thought that I could end up back here again sends me running in the other direction.

I see clearly and I am convicted this time to stay focused, too close to turn around.

What shall I do?

Where shall I go if my leadership requires me to stand in strength and confidence when I am weak and confused?

Whom can I turn too?

Lord have mercy!

My covering is unstable says he loves me and my son. His actions prove he is comfortable in not being a man of his word only to satisfy his self-prophetic word... *I'm a failure.* I see the dark spirits I hear the cry of his soul, but I cannot help him. You have warned me to let go! It's not like he doesn't know the clock is running out on this farce. Divorce is inevitable. I have waited too long to file the papers and cut away this dying flesh. I've had the papers, checked several times to verify what I needed to do, since the lapse in time from the first thought of divorce. Praying for a turn around, knowing deep in my soul this too is a set-up, and by the grace and mercy of God I make the right choice.

I sit in my comfortable pillowed black leather chair, while my promise rest his eyes through the night and the movie Titanic plays on the TV. Don't ask what month day or year it is. It could be any of the last 6 years I have been on this planet. I do not know if you call this a funk, ritual or fear. However, the staleness of this moment is depleting my energy. I feel like I am in purpose, but life seems to be a ritual.

Am I really cut out for this continual encouragement to others?

Is there one person I can call and just have a good conversation?

Not one person came to mind, because no matter who I call I will end up encouraging them or hearing their problems. Another night I sit alone. Married to a nonexistent husband my thoughts conjured up the days of my friends from past years. I have lost complete contact with all my friends, except one. In my attempt to remain in contact I am isolated... We talk but not sure it is from the heart. Alone I sit, at peace. It is either peace or numb. The fact is it's been painful and I've learned to just make do.

Is this surrender?

Have I given up, let go and pretended like I do not care for so long that I've thrown my hands up and said Lord I surrender with no understanding of surrender?

Lately surrender has been more than a close friend. He feels like a long standing guest that has an open ended invitation to come and go as he pleases.

Fulfillment still eludes me. I think it is filled with surrender. A very allusive state of being seems to appear at any point and time. Most time he shows up when things has not turned out the way I've anticipated or when a decision about what's my next move. Or it is dependant on the verdict of another's assessment of me being the perfect fit, worthiness or readiness of my desired accomplishment. *Mr. Surrender* not human but being human insist we have a close encounter. Our relationship is to initiate an easy release and will turn the tide of restlessness into an easy ride on the smooth ocean waves just like a skilled surfer.

I do not care what anyone says surrender is tough. Maybe it is the perception of what surrender represents. Defeat, denial, an uneven truce, succumbing or to be beaten by situation and circumstance.

Usually thrown around like Scooby snacks mostly in times when things are not going according to plan and after breaking down in tears in the midst of an enormous epiphany while watching the Queen of daytime talk shows,

I will not move forward until I am officially divorced.

My child asked me if I hurt myself, because the only time he has seen me cry like this is when I hurt myself or in church.

∞

To surrender means to relinquish, to yield to the power, control, or possession of another upon compulsion or demand: to give up completely or agree to forgo especially in favor of another: to give (oneself) up into the power of another especially as a prisoner: to give (oneself) over to something as an influence. To surrender, no wonder it is so tough.

Merriam Webster Dictionary

∞

Life, purpose, destiny, dreams, vision, love and even hate, faith and fear is ALL influenced by our ability to surrender. *My goodness!* There is no need to resist the inevitability of change in the process of life, purpose, destiny, dreams vision, love, faith hate and fear... How we internalize, interpret and embrace the process establishes the vibration for living a fulfilled life. Being numb or living life through filtered lenses of someone else's plan creates the persistence of an ineffective lackluster existence! Going through the motions never gaining any ground.

Am I a prisoner in life or for life?

Am I accommodating the power greater than me or pliable to the power that is in me created for me to forgo the demise— the ill-effect of my own thinking?

Am I strong enough to submit to THE SOURCE that created me in HIS likeness and after His image so that HIS WILL be done?

Or will my plans, agenda, schedules, list of items, things to do, outlines and schemes, and my programs out weigh HIS influence?

The song I surrender is echoing in my ears,

I surrender, I surrender ALL, I surrender I surrender ALL

ALL to Thee my precious Savior I surrender ALL!

∞

What a blessing to have my mother here with me. When you cannot help yourself the Lord will fix it where you have no choice but to follow His command. When my sexual appetite is at her peak I will not act on it because my mother is here.

Perhaps this is what Abraham felt when he and Sarah had not conceived their covenant child, drained, lifeless, and useless! Just going through the motions; nevertheless thanking God for an opportunity to be grateful in spite of the circumstances because of Gods faithfulness. I look at rerun movies for hidden messages that I may have missed in the second or third viewing; something that will reveal the next door I should open along with the key to open it. The truth is I am bored and not real sure of the outcome of my life. The only solace I have is my movies and a hope that it has got to get better.

A familiar place but not the same I am not the same woman from 10 years or even 6 years ago. Thank God. A few weeks ago I said to one of my spiritual sisters that one of the reasons I had not gotten divorced was that it was safe. I know it sounds crazy, but it is true. As long as I am still married I know nothing could or can happen because of my vows I would violate my commitment. That is how much I believe in marriage and commitment. It didn't matter my husband was absent, unfaithful, not available and in a reprobate state. The mere fact I had a husband meant I was not a woman who had a baby out of wedlock and I was not in the category of a single woman who had a baby, despite his father, my husband, was not present. Talk about insane in the membrane.

The cold truth is as long as I had an unstable man as the head of my natural family we would *always* be unstable. The mere fact he was never stable enough to take care of himself let alone us was a scary thought. I could not subject my child to his insecurities. A determination had to be made it was enough my son was the seed of an absent father but he carried the torch of setting a new paradigm for the men in his biological DNA. It was enough to divorce *Mr. who in the world are you?* and make a clear decision. You would think after watching my child say different men look like his Daddy, just because it was a man and he saw all the other boys at the park with their father it would be enough to cut the ties.

But to know that the rest of our days had the potential to be covered with poverty, scarcity, insecurity, reckless and fruitless living was more than enough for me to step into the other side of this journey and accept that the man I married was a part of my purpose, just not a part of my destiny.

How would I explain to my son about his father?

Will it be enough for him to have brothers around the church and community take time out with him and show him love and manhood?

Will I ever have the desire to re-marry?

Will I trust a mortal man again?

Will I trust myself with a man?

Or is my journey husbandless?

Whatever the case, I must circumcise this chapter of my life. Holding on to a nonfunctional, useless covenant was as bad as taking a placebo to cure cancer.

Is my only option to step into the present and embrace the future so that my child has a chance to live a life much different than his father?

I am sure if God can take Abraham from a familiar land to an unfamiliar; make him a promise that supersedes the stars in the sky; fulfill a promise and then bless the non-covenant child; surely he will make good on his promise to me.

∞

In Abraham's covenant a requirement of circumcision was mandated. Circumcision is the cutting a way of extra skin, flesh on every male child that was connected to Abraham. His voluntary obedience and responsibility to his faith in God's Word caused his ascent to the conditions of divine mercy. What I have learned in this journey is God will require us to cut away every fleshly connection that will hinder, distort or inhibit His promise coming to pass. This may be a marriage born out of fear, lust, and irresponsible intent. It could be friends that are not moving and flowing in the direction you are going; business connection that were inherited from a spirit of greed; and our own personal ideas, belief, motives that were not subdued to the Spirit of God. Anything that is not spiritually born or reborn will have to be circumcised as a result in obedience to God.

Ishmael was Abraham's first born; however as a requirement to receive the covenant, the promise, destiny he had to give his first-born back to God, a blood sacrifice. Lot was his family, and their came a cross road in his journey he had to let him go. Not because he didn't love him, but because the promise included a sacrifice, the sacrifice of blood. Because of his obedience to give it all up, he was in a position to make a request from God for Lot and Ishmael.

∞

"And as for Ishmael, I have heard thee: behold, I have blessed him, and will make him fruitful, and will multiply him exceedingly; twelve princes shall he beget, and I will make him a great nation."

Genesis 17:20

"And it came to pass, when God destroyed the cities of the plain, that God remembered Abraham, and sent Lot out of the midst of the overthrow, when he overthrew the cities in which Lot dwelt"

Genesis 19:29

∞

As it turns out my husband and most of my friends, a few of my close relatives and all of my business relationships had to be purged out of my life. Pride, fear, stubbornness and my will had to be turned completely over to the Lord of my life. My prayer began to reflect a desire of no harm to those I have grown to love:

Lord help us all with grace to let go and move on without major hurt disappointment and pain. Bless those who have mishandled my kindness, Bless those I have labored with only to find the very seeds I sowed were despised. Strengthen and fortify the weak places in my heart so I have the stamina to withstand challenges, dramatic changes, and uncertain times. Renew my confidence in you with ongoing assurance and faith that you will not leave me or forsake me by confirming and manifesting your promise through my obedience."

It was not easy. I did not want to feel alone or be alone. A very familiar cross and I did not want to bear it. My grandmother called one day and spoke encouraging words as she would from time to time,

"Go to Gethsemane."

O.k. granma what do you mean go to Gethsemane?

That is the place Jesus went to pray to seek God before he went to the cross.

I searched the scriptures and looked up the word Gethsemane. Gethsemane was a place where olive oil was pressed, a place of travail, and acceptance. History shows the best olive oils came from this part of the mountain. Of course olive oil was used for its medicinal healing properties—and the purer the better. In fact there are grades: virgin, extra virgin and extra-extra virgin. Gethsemane is the fork in the road, the final call before the final crossover. Jesus had to let go of his blood so that He would be the blood sacrifice for all. Power and cleansing is in His blood.

Similarly there are times when we have to let go of our blood in order to walk in the full power of His blood. Abraham was willing to make the ultimate sacrifice the blood of his covenant son Isaac. The ultimate test for Abraham was determining if he loved God more than the thing He promised him or gave him. Abraham's obedience God provided a way of escape: A ram in the thicket or tough place.

∞

"And Abraham lifted up his eyes, and looked, and behold, behind him a ram caught in a thicket by his horns: and Abraham went and took the ram, and offered him up for a burnt offering in the stead of his son"

Genesis 22:13

∞

Not only did God provide a way of escape, but he confirmed His promise again by an angel messenger....

∞

"And the angel of the Lord called unto Abraham out of heaven the second time,
And said, by myself have I sworn, say's the Lord: for because thou hast done this
That in blessing I will bless thee, and in multiplying I will multiply thy seed as the stars of the heaven, and as the sand, which is upon the seashore; and thy seed shall possess the gate of his enemies; And in thy seed shall all the nations of the earth be blessed, because thou hast obeyed my voice.

Genesis 22:15-18

∞

Can I let go of the promise so that I can receive the promise?

Will I hold on hoping that my faith will change another?

Is it my responsibility to believe for another like I believe for my bills to be paid and money to come to me now?

Can it be that belief is not faith, and that faith is the reality of what exists?

Perhaps our own denial in our will is a true testament of faith.

God is so incredible, marvelous, and magnificent. Last night I cannot believe that once again He confirmed His word. In our midweek service my Pastor taught on circumcision and cutting off those things that would hinder you from moving into your destiny or your next level experience with God. *Why continue tasting the goodness of God and never eating the fullness of His blessings.*

Wow!

Acutely aware I am in a place of revelation and practical living principles. God speaks to me through the Bible, next I get a living WORD, then the word is recalled in my Spirit, and after that He confirms the word through another person or situation.

My goodness!

Seek you first the Kingdom of God and all other things will be added becomes more than words they are now alive in me. As I turn from my will and yield myself to the Spirit of God, it often appeared to be a lonely path.

Why must I lose so much?

Is it really true the weight of God's glory will suffocate you if you are not prepared for it?

Is it true your gift will make room for you but your gift will not sustain you?

Is it You Again?...

Bishops, well known evangelists and pastors appeared to have public failure. The kind of wreckage that makes one scratch their head. It leaves you wondering how in the world could anyone preach, teach, encourage and inspire others in such anointing and revelation and be in a private, tore up mess. I knew little old parishioners like me could be that way. I knew a small time preacher could be a Holy Hot Mess, but not world renowned Ministers of the Gospel. If they had these kinds of problems what hope do I have?

Life experiences have a way of sobering you to deal with your junk. Life can force you to throw out the trash or become consumed and weighed down like human compose: used only for the life of others until you surrender to the power that created you. If there is no cutting away there can be no building up! The flesh cannot inherit Spiritual matters.

It will benefit from the Spirit; however, the flesh has been commanded to serve the Spirit. This means as the Spirit man is fortified the flesh, human will, desires, reactions to challenges, and experiences will be governed or guided from a spiritual place.

∞

"Stand fast, therefore, in the liberty with which Christ hath made us free, and be not entangled again with the yoke of bondage."

Galatians 5:1

∞

This was a time—while facing many obstacles and fears—I had to deal with my transformation and the acceptance of self, even in the face of an abusive and neglectful husband, stepping out in faith only to feel like I did not walk in enough faith, working with church folk again only to find out many are yet unappreciative and judgmental people who continually look for scapegoats for irresponsible behavior. I dealt with one disappointment after another, with only a brief moment of relief, wondering if *I am really on the right path.* Stamina had to be birthed. Stamina is the ability to withstand stay focused on the goal no matter what!

∞

"But they that wait upon the Lord shall renew their strength; they shall mount up with wings like eagles; they shall run and not be weary; and they shall walk and not faint."

Isaiah 40:31.

"For we wrestle not against flesh and blood, but against principalities, against powers the rulers of the darkness of this world, against spiritual wickedness in high places."

Ephesians 6:12

∞

Bull-dog tenacity became a reality as I relinquished myself to a Spiritual circumcision. Just like Rebecca, Isaac's wife I had two nations inside of me.

∞

Genesis 25:22-24

Verse 22 And the children struggled together within her; and she said, if it be so, why am I thus? And she went to inquire of the Lord.
Verse 23 And the Lord said unto her, two manner of people shall be born of thee; and the one people shall be stronger than the other people; and the elder shall serve the younger.
Verse 24 And when her days to be delivered were fulfilled, behold there were twins in her womb.

Paul put it this way, *"For the good that I would I do not; but the evil which I would not, that I do."*

Romans 7:19

∞

There were times I hoped my husband would change. I would pray,

Lord if he has not really made a change keep him away.

Every single time I prayed that prayer—and I do mean every time—I would get to the place of maybe we can come back under the same roof. Then, he would return to his first love Ms C! Things were so bad I did not even want him to touch me. My Soul, my mind had to relinquish the idea that I would be perpetuating a stigma and statistic and that my child would be fatherless. I had to let go that I may not have sex again for a while, I had to let go of my fear of being a single mother, I had to let go of my personal conversation of

How dumb could I be?

What was I thinking?

Why in God's name did I do this?

I had it all and gave it up for a reject!....

I had to let all of the schizophrenic conversation in my mind go so that my Spirit could serve my Soul. This meant I had to binge on the word of God; my life became ministry and taking care of my child. The only music I listened to for a long season was gospel and spiritual melodies. I overdosed on nothing but prayer and fasting until…the struggle over trusting God and obeying HIM became second nature or my new first nature. I had a new beingness and I did it without thought. I just did it!

When I wanted to hang out in anger, or with the desire to fulfill my physical needs, like sex, I asked God to help me where I couldn't help myself. Even when attempt to have a slip up reared his common head, a meeting or commitment would over take the arrangement. My entire life became my child, ministry and work. In that order…I would be so exhausted by the time I laid down I had no time to think about anything else.

Strong! Clear! And Precise! Isolated and alone I didn't realize my isolation and aloneness until I got still. Scripture says that God will make a way of escape from the snare or traps of the enemy. My escape was being surrounded with purpose. I made a calculated active choice to train like I was preparing for an Olympics marathon. My mind the very synapses were being altered to win the gold medal and nothing else would do.

Training is a lengthy process not an overnight trip unless one is willing to surrender to the process of being transformed. Merry-go-round living stifles the prize and intent of living a fulfilled life.

Not This Time

CONTRACTIONS

Ok. I think it is time…that was a real one,

We are hooking you to a monitor to watch your contractions, the nurse said. Oh see you just had a contraction.

 NO kidding…I looked at my husband as he looked at me. I do not need a machine to tell me when I am having a contraction, trust me I can feel every contraction…

The nurse, *oh that was a hard one…*

 I look at my husband again, *will someone please tell her I do not need her to narrate my pain!"*

He smiled; the nurse looked at him…

Ok, I will be back to check on you; we are calling your doctor.

Contraction is an action or process to bring on oneself especially inadvertently, incur: the state of being contracted : to establish or undertake by contract; to establish: to hire by contract : to limit restrict to knit, wrinkle: to draw together : to reduce to smaller size by or as if by squeezing or forcing together : to draw together so as to become diminished in size ; also to become less in compass, duration, or length: the shortening and thickening of a functioning muscle or muscle; a reduction in business activity or growth: a shortening of a word, syllable, or word group by omission of a sound or letter; also : a form produced by such shortening.

Merriam Webster Dictionary

∞

You may not remember this but I told you in the journey of *You Again?...* I desired to experience the same type of victory, miracles and blessings like they did in the Bible. What I did not realize was the entirety of the experience.

There is nothing like good sleep! It is a place where nothing else exists but you and your dreams. The average person does not remember what happens in their sleep or dream state. We all have them, most times more than one or two.

My child likes to invade my sleep with the words I love and hate to hear him say

"Mama, Mama..."

Followed by what ever question he has, which in most cases could have waited until I'd awakened. This can be most irritating early in the morning, either because I am not ready to wake up or enjoying a deep sleep. In his innocence of wanting whatever question answered at the time, he looks at me with the eyes saying,

"What's the problem, isn't it time to get up?!"...

This is what happens when God agitates us into action and change. He calls our name at the most awkward and uncomfortable times. He pulls on us to come out of our separation from him, a life segregated from purpose and destiny, the remoteness of our own agenda's, along with loneliness and seclusion of hiding out in fear. Out of deep sleep, apathy and nonchalant living, leaving your surroundings and atmosphere indifferent and lifeless to fulfillment!

He yanks us into dreams, visions, and aspirations—the kind of stuff that obviously cannot be accomplished without Him. Then He inserts and ignites a flame of irresistible favor! He constricts you to focus and discipline until the manifestation of Divine purpose. Partitions of our blasé thinking, which inhibit the sweet flow of a fulfilled life, are burned away.

In the spirit of fulfillment and Divine Connections contractions are experienced!

Previously I gave the definition of contractions. In the experience of spiritual birth and maturity, contractions are the action or process to bring on oneself (especially inadvertently) into occurrence and incurrence with Divine alignment: the state of being contracted: The journey to establish or undertake by contract or covenant promise that establishes *full – fill–meant.*

We are limited and restricted in our mobility and knitted together in relationship with our Creator, wrinkled only to reveal the refreshing of our spirit in His Spirit. Our world is drawn together to reduce to a smaller existence and size by squeezing or forcing together Mind– Soul– Will with the Spirit of God. Our verbal communication is shortened and limited to only push and omit sounds, letters, and intransitive verbs that would stimulate the flow of destiny. We must draw together with God so pride and ego cannot destroy and bring a reproach to the beauty in us not yet revealed in the physical world. What we encounter, the duration; our length of stay in this intense restriction is totally predicated on our ability not to complain during the reduction in busyness activities or growth.

What does this mean?

It is painful, constricting and downright agonizing at times to live a fulfilled life. But the reward is Opulence, Affluence, Luxury, Elegance, FREEDOM and the ability to instigate real transformation creating a world of true Spiritual harmony different than anything you or I have witnessed in the earth to date.

God called us to an Old Fashion All Night Prayer. Little did I know birth would take place into a new Spiritual dimension; Twelve midnight I literally begin feeling contractions as if I were in labor. I was praying I began asking God,

What is this?

In that moment an Elder got up,

"We started this prayer on the 31st and now it is the 1st day of the 9th month and we have been birthed into a new dimension of abundance and spiritual freedom..."

My God, I thought …

Cramping along with physical contractions was intensified. I had to sit down.

Continuing praying speaking in my heavenly language under my breath, he continued....

"This is why it has been so hard.... This is why the last few months have been so uncomfortable and difficult... God is saying you have made it into this new realm of existence and living in his kingdom."

This may sound very ethereal. However, whatever you believe, I am sure you can make the connection that all things in the universe go through a phase of birthing. The process of being pregnant with a child, dream, idea, change, and or a flower blooming has to burst out of a seed and then in the right season year after year a new rose pushes out of a tight bulb.

Depending on how, when and where the rose is planted and if it was nurtured and protected properly in the winter months a beautiful rose bush will emerge. Growth is in stages. Each stage or cycle causes some form of discomfort and adjustment.

∞

"For the whole creation/earth groans and travails in pain together until now."

Romans 8:22

"And not only they (all creation/earth) but ourselves also who have the first fruits of the Spirit even we

ourselves waiting for the adoption, the redemption of our body."

Romans 8:23

"For we are saved (set Free) by hope, but hope that is seen is not hope; for what a man sees why does he hope for it?"

Romans 8:24

"But if we hope for that which we see not, do we with patience wait for it."

Romans 8:25

"Likewise the Spirit also helping our infirmity, for we know not what we should pray as we ought, but the Spirit itself makes intercessions for us with groaning which cannot be uttered."

Romans 8:26

"And he that search the heart know what is the mind of the Spirit itself make intercession for the saints according to the will/purpose of God."

Romans 8:27

∞

I gave birth to FREEDOM! Restoration! All of the years of lack, frustration, and choices made in fear, the creation of Ishmael out of impatience, the stagnation of other peoples problems and crisis, which I internalized and made my problems, unproductive actions, idle words and business ventures into pain and aches manifested themselves in my physical body. I stepped into the Full-Fill-ment of DESTINY.

The ninth year anniversary of a pivotal time in my life, reflection of where I was 9-years ago reminded me I was in the belly of fear, because of my inability to embrace and accept my purpose and destiny. This was how I ended up in Murfreesboro, Tennessee with Mr. Sincere. Now I was in a valley giving birth to another promise. The promise of never returning to my past living in the present with a future not yet realized or experienced.

What usually happens when I am in quest for answers I seek God with an open declaration show me and give me a confirmation that is clear an unmistaken. When Elder opened his mouth with the words I was not going to say this but I have too. *"We started this prayer on the 31st and now it is the 1st day of the 9th month and we have been birthed into a new dimension of abundance and spiritual freedom"*

I received a confirmation! God answered my request of confirmation and clarity. Luke 1:13-25 and 1:34-47 became a real experience for me just like with Zacharias and Elisabeth; and then, as Elisabeth was a witness or confirmation to Mary and Joseph Luke 1:34-47.

∞

∞

Elder confirmed what was being birthed through my Spirit.

"We started this prayer on the 31st and now it is the 1st day of the 9th month and we have been birthed into a new dimension of abundance and spiritual freedom"

My work, my dream, my hope was all being challenged by strife, envy and rebellion each effort, step forward, and move in the direction to seeing Gods promise fully manifested was connected to people and circumstances who seemed to breed some type of constant, persistent, strain, growth and then decline.

Fortunately I was able to see above the dense fog to a safe place and a determination not to return to familiar refuge. *"Mr. Trick"* *the person who looks good, sounds good but in your belly you know it is a one way ticket to heartbreak and disappointment* and *"Mr. I don't think so" is the person who obviously you wouldn't fall for but an attempt is made anyway to see if you have weakened* resurfaces periodically, but where I didn't have the strength to say no, I was so busy I had no time to get fooled by *Mr. Trick* or *Mr. I don't think so.* My home and child became my safe haven. In quietness I learned to worship and praise God, independent of being in a congregation or the fellowship of other Believers. I reacquainted with my old friend, the Bible. We made up for some real good conversation. Studying and nurturing my dream and teaching my child to do the same. Even when I wanted to go for the counterfeit and trust me there were times when the counterfeit looked, sounded and could have felt like a good trick and treat but I learned to stay focused. Through pure exhaustion, I could not do anything else; talk about an escape from my worst enemy: Me!

Through all of the convulsions, contractions, wilderness and valley experiences I learned to nurture and protect my gift. Develop the muscle of *no* and *not this time.* I learned to totally embrace my inner knower, pay attention to flashing neon red signs and subliminal dialogues that can only be heard in truth not facts.

∞

"When I am in conflict with self and my mind debates between what I want and what my body craves or thinks she is missing, when my Spirit encourages me to hold on I have no choice but to resort to a Power that is greater than my will power. I pull on the supernatural power of my God, the creator of the universe, the one who made me through His one breath of life. He breathed into my dead and dusty soul and said live! Suddenly, I find the strength to refocus and not make a phone call to relieve my tension; I pull my mind and will under the rule and sovereign monarch authority in the Kingdom of God. I remember my inheritance and choose not to forfeit my birth right with a temporary fix. I choose not to act like an orphan with no place to call home. I choose not to waste the precious time redeemed to me with frivolous actions and spiritual abortions.

Yes, in my insane moment and momentary lapse of memory I try to satisfy my overwhelming urge of relief— a temporary fix—only to be protected by an angel. The unseen hand of God creates escapes and paths for me to take that will help me avoid what lays in the far recesses of my memory banks. "

∞

After giving birth, I was in a valley, desert, and an incubating stage. The ride was worse than an air flight hitting a turbulent thunder storm. Have you every clinched your teeth with the anticipation of distracting or disturbing news? Unaware that you are holding your breath, not breathing, no oxygen is entering your brain and neither is the poisonous carbon dioxide leaving your body. A stand off, waiting for a signal that it is ok to breathe, only to find that this auto-response to stress has created hyper sensitive teeth to cold or heat. Everything that enters your mouth has to be swished around like a blender before it hits the back of your mouth and teeth. Or else the sharp dull pain that lingers for a bleeping moment leaves a lasting impression on your memory banks of not again?

I never had teeth or mouth problems but after giving birth to my son I noticed my teeth were not as strong. Brushing my teeth one morning one tooth chipped; also I have noticed unconsciously throughout the day and in my sleep I clinch my jaw pressing down on my back teeth. I could not figure out why all of a sudden my back teeth and jaw line were so sensitive. Then one day I realized I was clinching my teeth and not breathing. Now, I am aware of stress and I actively choose to release, Inhale and Exhale.

It is said while pregnant your baby will get whatever he or she needs from your body either by pulling from reserves in your body or diet. In spite of attempting to control my stress level while pregnant, apparently I was extremely stressed.

Life will sneak into the same mode of auto protection before you know it. Your every move is protected with the over stimuli of "I can't, I shouldn't." The last time I reached for more than getting up in the morning, eating, working or eating, taking care of others or eating and sleeping I failed. I have seen this before, the plain old "I don't think so!" It was too painful.

Like a blender, our dream gets crushed into unidentified ice flakes that melt into tasteless liquid giving just enough to survive; disturbing, distracting, disappointments; trying to get "People" to join our campaign of a life of more when all they want is to survive. This is what happens with *the church people.* The experience of church, ministry becomes an escape to deal with the grim reality of a mundane life. Anything that pushes church people out of a *"I-am-ok-you-are-too-saved?"* excuse ridden lifestyle, will instigate the blame game.

The blame game leaves church people comfortable with being void and empty. Temporary fixes and highs, I knew it existed just didn't realize how complacent and comfortable church folk get in religious dogma. I was committed to purpose, a *spiritual revolution,* among *the church people*; and, anytime your purpose is attached to transforming the thinking of years, generations of recycled behavior that has produced generations of poverty, sicknesses, and mental imprisonment, trust me you are a target for strife, envy and a down right rebellion.

Evaluating ones perception of God and how God may choose to show up in life and circumstances of life is not comfortable. Prodding *the ground of confinement* to move God out of the confinement of personal thoughts; or limiting Him to finite ideas and interpretation of what our experience with the Holy Spirit should be or how the infinite source of God chooses to reveal abundance is like finding a needle in a hay stack *in the church people.*

By all means do not define the freedom of God as not being bound to man's traditions that are laced with biblical text or a wish list and what we sometime call miraculous intervention is not the only relationship God wants to have with us. Talk about a rift in the fabric of church. Attempting surgery on cataract ridden eyes for an EYE opening experience going beyond the limits of mere existence to a world reflecting God in our collective efforts is like doing surgery with no anesthesia. Unless one is tired of being tired, and tired of talking about being tired, neither willing to blame or relinquish responsibility to false hope, humility and happiness for how they experience this magnificent world given to us and leave the institution of ill ineffective thinking, all one can do is let them be.

Maybe I am crazy, but was it not Jesus death and resurrection that confronted those who crucified him?

Was it not He who declared it is finished and then the collective existences of mankind at that time realized in their presence was a true King, Priest and the Son of God?

Partial embracing of biblical teaching is the real culprit to seeing transformation in daily existence. Yes, there has been a great deal of mishandling of the gospel, and an argument could be sustained with facts that this is what has created what I call The Paranoid Debate, which is when scripture is used to justify actions and lack of integrity with our word and commitment.

One of my favorite cop-out lines that I have heard, over and over is,

"God has released me from that assignment"

The truth is most times we have left the assignment mentally long before verbal acknowledgements I know longer want to do this are uttered. For whatever reason, the bottom line is we all get tired, do not like some of the things we see, neither do we agree with everything we hear, *but to what and who are we committed?*

Are we clear?

Do we trust God to help us in the time of need and to do what we cannot in our own humanity?

Do we trust He is a man of his word: proven, full of integrity and quite clear on his agreement with us?

If not careful the born-again believer can start operating like a fictionalized wizard; using the Bible like a magic wand. Manipulating The Word to fit our inability to go through the process of faith, using His promises, patterns and agreements, just like a televised witch. Pulling out a formula stirring a little feel good music and fall out emotions, creating an illusionary anointing full of mist, haze, and vapor, a fog that is laced with bargaining tools not authorized in the Kingdom of God or influenced by the substance of God.

We become the walking comatose, not only are eyes open wide shut but we serve in ministry for years, go to church, pray and fast, do not do anything openly wrong… and our attitudes become stones of do not rock my boat. Living has to be more than survival, on my way to heaven and glad about it, but full of the desire to embrace all of God's promises, heaven and the Kingdom of God in the earth. At the other end of the spectrum is, of course Jesus' challenged the traditional thinkers in the synagogue and they called him a heretic.

Maybe it is a fact the initial process to living a fulfilled life is laboring. You know the scripture didn't say it wouldn't be "work" or constraints. What he said, is *"my yoke is easy and burden is light" Matthew 1: 29-30,* which means the benefits of surrendering to the constraints of His will instead of our own agenda, plan, and things to do is easier and light by comparison.

∞

"Take my yoke upon you and learn of me; for I am meek and lowly in heart and you shall find rest unto your soul; for my yoke is easy and my burden is light."

Matthew 1:29-30

∞

Could it be the abnormal areas of our life which we embrace as normal causing conflict in embracing true Spiritual principles? More often than I would care to admit unadulterated Spiritual principles are viewed as farfetched, unreal and unattainable. Operating in daily survival suffocates harmony, authentic peace and free flowing abundance. Our accustomed, learned way of being leans toward the norm or dominant rule of society, not the normal, all powerful rule of sovereignty.

Once upon a time I thought it was the preacher's, pastors, and leader's full responsibility which created a one-sided infected church dynamic governed by the politics of this world. Now after being fully committed to living in fulfillment and on the other side of ministry in the church as a leader and a witness to true men and women who have a true heart for people, giving the now, uncut, revelations of God, I have come to see that the entanglement of pride and the oppression of the mind and will, causes and creates a distorted view of what rebellion to the true essence of God really is.

∞

Maybe this is why you could not receive me in my rawness, uncooked and rare state. It was too much for you. I get it. The scripture says Jesus came to His own people and His own received him not. Meaning he did not come as a scholar, a priest although he was, he did not come in religious dogma, traditions and rituals even though He knew the traditions. He came to fulfill the law, decree, command and rule. Jesus came in the volume of the book—the frequency of the Word—and only those who knew the word or the frequency of HIS word could hear His voice.

∞

"Then said I, Lo, I come in the volume of the book it is written of me to do thy will O God."

Hebrew 10:7

∞

"And when he put forth his own sheep, goes before them and the sheep follow him; for they know his voice

St. John 10:4

"And a stranger will they not follow, but will flee from him: for they know not the voice of strangers."

St. John 10:5

"My sheep hear my voice, and I know them and the follow"

St. John 10:27

The *worldly* are not indoctrinated in the hereafter. They have a sense of *"in this life we are to enjoy the fruits of our labor – have a few pleasures and be happy."* This fact enables the *worldly* to embrace basic Spiritual principles with a little more ease and less rebellious motives. They understand you do A, to get B; you follow the pattern, you will get the results. *The church people* on the other hand grapple over *why, doesn't make sense, who died and made you God,* and on and on.

Consolation of *"here and now vs. here and after (heaven)"* is used as a badge of honor to be loose with our commitments. Through word and lack of discipline we consistently and inappropriately apply our promise in every area of our life as we are being attacked by Satan. The truth is we lack integrity with our commitments.

When the goal is to get our reward in the after life the objective becomes just to get by and be comfortable enough to make it to heaven. Church, Ministry, The Bible becomes a crutch not to try anything or go beyond waking up, eating, working, taking care of others, eating, homework, church, eat and sleep. It is what we use to sedate us from living life now.

Anticipation, expectations and excitement and the newness of a new born child quickly becomes consumed with the uncomfortable, adjustments, sleepless nights, constant monitoring and feeding. The first four to eight weeks are spent in isolation; the initial immunity and protection of your child has to be guarded. Add to this picture existing responsibilities: bills, if you have other children tending to their needs, a husband or wife, perhaps work outside the home, and so on. The newborn is now a weighty responsibility. You love your new child and there are moments of pleasure as you watch your child grow. As your child is more aware of surroundings and etc… each stage of development presents new adjustments and challenges. This is not a comfortable place, but the reward is great.

Ironically, the interpretation of Revelation 12th Chapter in the Bible gives us this exact pattern —Rejoice, ye heavens you *men and women transformed by the renewing of your min* and warning to the inhibitors of the earth and the sea –*men and women not transformed by the renewing of your mind*–For *strife, rebellion, and envy* is come down unto you, having great wrath because he know that he hath but a short time!

When the *one carrying wrath* saw that he was *not allowed to inhabit the promise* he persecuted *the one giving birth to promise or has given birth to promise.*

To you who have given birth to promise you are given *the ability to soar above chaos, the storm and see through the dense fog* that you might fly into a *safe haven* a place where you are nourished for a time– you will *breathe The Word of God and the building of your faith* from the face of *deception,*

The deceiver will cast out of his mouth– *Words to slash the integrity, character and authority* against you that he might cause you to be *destroyed by the strife, rebellion and envy.*

The dry place produced men and women who spoke the word like Ezekiel 37 and swallowed up the Oxygen of strife, rebellion and envy.

Strife, rebellion and envy is angry with you *the producer of the promise* and wants to make war with the *those left standing and breathing the promise: Manifestation of the promise*, who keep the commandments of God and have the testimony of Jesus Christ: *Walking, living and breathing the promise.*

∞

"The nature of evil is that it lives in realms beyond itself. So it is hard to get a handle on it because it goes down here and sprouts up over there. It affects us all, so the peacemaker might become violent because so much violence is around him or her."

Dr. Maya Angelou

∞

Our Spiritual fulfillment is predicated on the same pattern as giving natural birth. It is the ability to do the necessary work. We must allow a time of isolation and guarding of one's heart, dreams and purpose, monitoring what we are feeding our Spirit, soul and mind. We are ever conscious of our commitment to not allow strife, rebellion and envy to linger in any form in our thinking, so that God's full promise can be released in our daily lives.

Not This Time

THE FULFILLMENT

Not This Time

SHUT UP

"Sometimes it is best not to say anything",

my mother...

"The loudest one in the room is the weakest one in the room",

Lucas in the movie American Gangster...

"I have encouraged myself and I encourage others to tell the truth. However, there is this: you don't have to tell everything you know. When you are questioned be direct and brief and truthful. Just tell the truth."

Dr. Maya Angelou

∞

Not This Time

∞

*"In the multitude of words there is sin, but he that
refrain his lips is wise"*

Proverbs 10:19...

*"Because I do not say anything, does not mean I do not
have anything to say."*

iRiS

∞

I have learned that silence, being quiet, stillness, taking a holy hush moment can sometime speak louder than any spoken word. It is an art in refraining from addressing every no, yes, maybe, falsehood, truth, trumped up charges, or fact.

Facing bankruptcy, not just a financial bankruptcy but an emotional and spiritual depletion; the kind of soul depravation when you haven given all, you have done all and it appears you are still coming up short, misunderstood, and dreams look far fetched.

Travelling Summerlin Parkway in Las Vegas, Nevada, on my way to church telling God how tired I was, what I didn't like about Las Vegas, how I didn't come here to live like a pauper, my baby daddy not helping with Similac or Pampers, people lying on me, struggling to pay my rent, I owe everybody, I had good credit when I moved here now I cannot get credit...need to get my car serviced, tags are due, just going on and on ... and I heard Shut-Up… I looked in my rearview mirror to see if it was my child, I thought to myself,

"He has lost his mind I will pull this car over and whoop his butt!"

Guess what, he was asleep…

I don't know if this has ever happened to you. Some people call this schizophrenia. I continued to drive, and I heard…

"Walk through this. This is not passing and the longer you complain the longer it will take…"

It was the voice of wisdom, or of God. I know this because I had heard my pastor teach this and I personally studied for myself. The Bible talks about being able to guard your mouth and heart so your life or promise of life is kept. So, when he taught the word in church the word was in me, the seed was planted and it surfaced in my thinking—or my Spirit reminded me of what God had spoken regarding complaining…

I took a deep breathe and reluctantly said,

Okay. Tears welled in my eyes.

∞

"He that keeps his mouth keeps his life, but him that open wide his lips shall have destruction.

Proverbs 13:3

∞

Working in ministry during the day, and at Kinko's at night; had to move from one unit in my apartment complex to a less expensive unit, taking care of my child, and still did not have enough to take care of basic needs. I applied and interviewed at the Venetian Hotel and Resorts on The Strip in Las Vegas. Hired in my specialty as a Corporate Trainer I attended the orientation only to have my supervisor tell me I'd be working 12 – 14 hour days and the childcare center did not have room for my child.

At that moment, I thought I was looking at the first building of the World Trade Center blow up in New York as I sat and watched my television in California. Just like that! Highjacker's blew up my monument of security, my reliance on my ability to get a job, make money and save the day. What was once security was lying in front of me like the ashes from 9/11 I thought I was going to get relief and now I looked at ruins, non replaceable ruins. This meant I could not keep the job.

The relief I thought I was getting could not happen. I was right there only to see it slip through my hands. Once again I felt the sting of Ishmael in my life. The desire to run tried to rear his ugly head.

Go back to LA…

Like there was something waiting for me in LA, I guess it was a continued nightmare. The next familiar test was a man. Good conversation and innocent flirtation…the more we talked I realized this was a trick, not that he was a bad person…but where was this really going…NoWhere…but around the same mulberry bush if I did not choose differently.

I had been through too much to turn back and knew the innocent trick and refused to eat at his table. I laughed at what old people would say,

"There is nothing new under the sun"

Same trick, new day, new characters…I do not think so! I thought. The muscle of discipline was getting a good work out.

∞

"The soul of the sluggard desire and has nothing; but the soul of the diligent shall be made fat"

Proverb 13:4

∞

August 7, 2006 is etched in my memory. It is the date before I knew about the re-invasion of cancer in my mothers' body a total stranger introduced herself as a messenger.

∞

"Daughter this is the year of many shifts and changes. Trust in me with all your heart, and do not lean to your understanding. In all your ways acknowledge Me, and I

will show myself strong on your behalf. I will make your way straight as you wait on Me. I will grant you sound wisdom and counsel from above, but you must turn your ear toward Me completely. I will bless you beyond your wildest imaginations if you will trust Me completely.

This is a time to return to your first love and to put Me first beyond all else. This is a time for worship, prayer, and listening as you meet with Me. Turn away from all that distracts you, and lean unto Me, for I have great things to reveal to you as you draw into My presence. If you trust in the grace that has lingered upon you from years gone by and continue in distraction, then your light will grow dim and your influence will weaken for it is only in Me that you find life, strength, and light. It is dangerous for you to fail to return to your first love, but it is life to you if you draw close. I am waiting for you. I am longing for you.

Only in My presence will you find understanding and strength. Many voices will say to you go this way or that way, but as you listen for My voice alone, you will find the wisdom that you long for. You will hear Me say, "This is the way, walk in it! Those who wait upon me shall be clothed with power from on High.

Those who wait for My word will experience break-through!

If you humble yourself in this season, you will experience fresh empowerment in the next. If you meet with Me in the secret place in this season, you will be greatly rewarded in the next. My promise to you is for expansion, enlargement, fruitfulness, and increase.

Come, My daughter, into My presence and I will reveal things to you that your eye have not yet seen, that your ears have not heard, and neither has it even entered your heart. Come into

My presence and I will fill you with My counsel. Come into My presence, and I will empower you. Come into My presence, and I will prosper you. You are my delight, and I will raise you up in this hour if you lean upon Me."

∞

Finally, talked my mother into moving to Las Vegas, she had been in Las Vegas maybe a month or two. In her amazement she did not know how in the world I was functioning with the schedule I was keeping. All, I could say nothing but Gods grace. I knew that I was functioning only because of God and definitely not on or in my own will or power. On the other hand I knew something was going on with the health of my mother, just didn't know what.

I gave a two week resignation notice to Kinko's and during the two weeks my mother took a trip to California to visit her brother who lay in a hospital in a coma. On her way to the hospital while in California she missed a step on the porch and slipped and fell down on the porch of my grandmother's house. Nothing seemed apparently wrong at the time.

The next day she was immobile… Rushed to the hospital
diagnosis was unclear—pneumonia, cancer, bronchitis—
just unclear my sister and I were traumatized.

Not This Time

Not This Time

NOT WHAT I EXPECTED

What do you do when you have waited on God to deliver and heal, but his choice of deliverance is not quite what you expected?

∞

"Hope deferred makes the heart sick. But when the desire comes, it is a tree of life."

Proverbs 13:12

Not This Time

∞

*G*rief *swallowed each second of my days and night; Endless sadness! It felt like Hurricane Katrina. We were warned of the outcome but not prepared for the final blow and spread of cancer in my mother's body. I'm not sure anything could have prepared us for the typhoon of emotions we had yet to encounter.*

Our hope was the worst was over. Only to learn a new storm had just begun in spite of the facts we were still recouping from the last barrage of physical and emotional tirade.

Sorrow filled my heart and flooded my soul, my mind. A whirlwind of emotions I couldn't have been prepared for. Constant mourning, brief breaks from remembrance and sadness. I am functioning. I think. It is the fourth month and last month my Pastor declared in a message he preached. We must follow the instructions of the Lord to the letter. I thought what else do you want God? I have done all I know to do! In my desperation I thought again, Early Morning Prayer, without thought I announced effective tomorrow Monday we will begin 6:30 am prayer Monday thru Friday.

June 26, 2009 Michael Jackson left this world unexpectedly. I turned the television from all news as if I thought not hearing the news of Michael's death would falter and change the outcome of my mothers deteriorating body. She lay in bed unable to move, talk or eat. Nurses visited our home, each saying they did not expect her to make it through the weekend. This happened the entire month of June until her death. They encouraged us to prepare ourselves. I think we heard those words we saw the decline but had an unspoken hope Mama will get up from this bed. Then the news of Farrah Fawcett, another celebrity whom had been in the news, battled one the rarest of rare cancers, rectal. Her openly two year battle ended in a fatal blow with death.

A typhoon of loneliness invaded my daily activities without invitation. Often treated as if I had a plague my companion, the one I talked to. The one who tolerated my moods and frustrations without judgment, gone! I yet battle with the thought "would I have preferred her here in sickness than not to have her here healthy?" Pretty scary thought to think I could possibly be that selfish.

Is it money that makes the difference in handling grief?

Is it how close you are to the one you loose?

Janet Jackson says what has kept her going is staying busy. She is releasing a new album, released the first video from the album, completed a movie, has been seen at all of the High Fashion shows is Milan, New York etc… in the last 4 months and she looks darn good.

Is part of my grief I do not know how I am going to take care of my child?

I have placed applications all over Las Vegas, Los Angeles, created new training classes, have not been paid on work I've already completed. Not in a position to move, not in a position to stay just a mess!

When my mother took ill exactly little more than two years ago, the diagnosis and prognosis was grim. The oncologist described her as a delicate flower needing much care and attention, her chemotherapy treatment would start slow. So, from May 2007 until the end of June 2007 my mother went from unconscious to conscious, from pneumonia to gall stones, to the truly unexpected Lung Cancer! Breast cancer metastasized to the lung.

Devastated but not faithless, we made sure we had things lined up in the untimely event my mother was chosen to depart this life and the instantaneous breath we take for granted was stopped.

Faith! Was it Faith or pure unwillingness to deal with the cards dealt?

Can we deal with the cards dealt in practical wisdom and yet hold on to our faith that with God all things are possible?

Are we consumed with the overwhelming, uncontrolled emotions pulling us out of the realm of existing in a manner that doesn't produce added grief and sorrow?

It was never my mother's desire or intention to leave us with debt. In fact, her dream, her fight was to leave an inheritance for her children. Many of her desires laid locked up inside of her chasing and believing in the faithless; those things and most of all people undeserving of her faith.

I suspected her health was much worse than she let on, but I never thought cancer until I saw how she breathed in her sleep; an indescribable peaceful gasp with each inhale and exhale. I had seen that look before; in a close friend of the family, a look of breathing death. A disfiguring aging mouth droops while in sleep, lifeless gasping for air with each intense *Inhale* and *Exhale*.

Later I asked my mother if she had the doctors do an x-ray of her chest. I do not think she ever gave me a straight answer. I have tried to remember her response, but it is unclear. I think she said when she went back to California she would have them do another chest x-ray.

Bronchitis, deep coughing all signs of something more serious than a passing flu cured with antibiotic or plain ole' father time. God only knew something much worse was brewing and festering in my mother's body. January 2007 she had 5 years clean of breast cancer and supposedly she didn't have to return for another year for a check-up. There were times I would speak to my mother over the phone and her voice was weak. Sometimes she said she stayed in for days, not like her at all. My mom was very active. Finally she made the decision to move to Las Vegas with my sister and me.

After moving out of her condo, she stayed in a hotel room for a couple of weeks. She called late one Saturday night very ill.

"I can't explain it", she said.

"I am weak, and just sick!"

I asked if she wanted me to call 911 or call someone to come and check on her.

"No, I think if I lay down a little while I will be alright."

Thinking back on that night, I wondered why she called me. I was too far away to do anything. However, her body was obviously letting her know something is wrong and she knew it, just didn't know how to face it. I prayed with her. We hung up and thirty minutes later I called to check on her. She was a little better.

Was it the ceiling dropping in her condo from the overflow of water from the upstairs unit?

Was it mildew and asbestos that aggravated the disease?

She mentioned a shot the doctor had given her for arthritis and she seemed to think her body was not the same after.

Was it the shot?

To add insult to injury she returned home to California to check on her brother because of an accident he had and landed him in a coma in the hospital only to end up in the hospital herself.

A simple slip, on the steps, on the porch, of her mother's home put her in the hospital the following day.

∞

"A time to be born and a time to die..."

Ecclesiastes 3:2

"...and it is appointed for men to die once..."

Hebrews 9:27

∞

Did the dream of millions inhibit the obvious or was it really Faith?

I weep today for my mother, my child, myself. Perhaps secretly I am afraid I may turn out like my mother. Work hard, Give Hard, Love Hard and in the end Die Hard, Peaceful but hard.

It is a hard death when you are in place of unfulfilled dreams. You may have experienced a lot of the joys of life, but true fulfillment of dreams always seemed to almost be there. Then you are faced with the prognosis of an early death.

She never questioned the faithfulness of God. She was surprised of the final turn out in her health. She was grateful for the additional time given her. Her physical body was weak she even took responsibility for not being specific enough with her request from God. She said, I should have been a tad bit more thorough in my request,

"I asked Him to bless me to get insurance perhaps I should have asked that I stayed around long enough for my children to get my insurance."

In her frailty she was yet concerned about her children. Not wanting to leave a burden.

I drive the interstate and get a flash of a woman in a casket. It's my mother! She doesn't look like my mother; I remember the feelings of shock, numbness, and OMG! Death is cold! Our flesh is truly a shell an empty house unless breath, spirit, soul is flowing in our veins. It's Empty! My Mother IS NOT HERE!

Then it switches to the makeover.

Still no real comfort because she's cold and clammy, slight smile but her big, beautiful eyes will never open. I will never hear her say, *Lurindaaaaa!* That is what she called me. She will never give me the Mama look. You know the look.

We have nothing with her voice except for a little video that shows her in her fight, she is sending a birthday greeting to my brother-n-law. The memories have stopped with death and I cannot seem to get beyond her cold body!

I try to breathe but I find myself holding my breathe: Bracing myself for the next windfall, not knowing if or how I can deal with anything else. Will I be able to continue? Can I carry the mantle she has left for me? What legacy will I create of her life? I weep at the thought she will not be here Thanksgiving. She will never bake another cake, cook another roast, turkey, ox-tails, bean soup, oh, and her greens. She will not fry another chicken; make another rice dressing, or plain old-fashioned corn bread dressing, and her potato salad, macaroni and cheese, string beans, fresh snap peas, okra corn and tomatoes. She tossed a salad that made a person who says,

"I don't like that"

Come back for seconds. And do not let me forget the cornbread hot water corn bread and then she would make me one of my favorites: lima beans. Yeah she could cook lima beans that would just melt in your mouth. Sweet corn soufflé, sweet potato soufflé—oh my! I am getting hungry thinking about my mama's cooking…Hey, go figure her food is putting a smile on my face. Short ribs hum! hum! hum!

I am learning the test of our faith truly comes again and again, the intensity of the test changes as you grow in faith.

After a two and a half year battle with the reoccurrence of cancer; being told on three distinct separate occasions my mother would not make it through the night. I saw the hand of God not only get her through the night but miraculously strengthen her to not only get out of the hospital but walk again.

This time was different. She had a seizure induced stroke. Later it was determined to be the spreading of the dreadful, ugly deteriorating disease cancer. This time the cancer found its way to her brain, spine and in her bones.

The Sunday prior to this particular Monday, she had desired to go to church. She had missed a couple of Sunday's and wanted to go. But her body was too weak. In fact the last service she attended it was obvious she fought with everything within her to hold herself up in the seat.

This particular Sunday, she mustered enough strength to sit on the side of the bed with desire but only the strength of tears. I am just not going to be able to make it.

"Do you want to eat?" I asked,

"No baby, not right now" and she lay back down.

I saw the weakness in her face, I saw the battle to be strong wither into the confidence that if God don't do something, it will not be done.

She insisted I go on to church. Immediately after service I called. Her voice weak and frail,

"Baby, I am so weak..."

Did you eat the food I left?

"No baby, just come home…"

"Ok, I am on my way."

She cried when I arrived, I prayed and encouraged her best I could and then was able to get her to eat a little. My sister came by and she got a little relief from the ravishing effects of cancer in her body. We had our Sunday afternoon ritual, talked, laughed, looked at TV and slept.

Monday, morning I arose to give her yogurt and found she was still asleep. But, it was getting late and I knew she had to get up

"…Mom, here are your morning meds and your yogurt"

"Ok, baby leave it on the table, I will get it."

We had a bedside table for her. I left the room, went in the living room with my son, like I often do, turned on the computer to do some work and my son says,

"Nanny is calling you."

I listen, run to her room and I am in shock! My mother appears to be having a seizure/stroke.

How could it be? How could what we thought was stabilizing now be growing in a way that is not only inoperable, but, according to the doctors, gives a death sentence for sure.

Alarming news and the hysterics of feeling betrayed by oncologists sent rage and fury through my veins. There are multiple tumors on my mother's brain and one that is in a position where if not hindered from growing would not only leave my mother a vegetable, but mentally incompetent unable to talk, feed herself, go to the restroom on her own. What I did not know is that she would be completely aware and just unable to express herself.

Two weeks of radiation, to shrink and slow the process of death and improve the quality of her life while this raging disease ate away at her like piranhas tear away at a fresh batch flesh.

Approximately a year earlier I had raced to my sister's home due to the unsettling certainty that the probability of our mother living another year was not likely. "We need to prepare," I said because this time next year I do not think mother will be here. These words echoed from my memory bank as I watched my mother's physical strength waste away. Amazingly her face maintained a glow, not a wrinkle, just feeble flesh. Before leaving the hospital a social worker attempted to sooth the process of death. The worker recommended hospice care, of course we would not hear of it.

Hospice gave the scent of giving up, releasing my mother to the other side. We were just not ready for that. It was tough; we yet believed her healing would take place on this side of the mountain. Her quiet demeanor was not only obvious but unnerving. My mother always said God let's you know when your time on earth is ending and her quietness was as if she knew her time was ending.

Mothers Day 2009 my mother was in the hospital. The second time in her life she spent Mothers Day in the hospital with unfavorable prognosis. The first time was two years earlier and now again. Exactly two years later. The cancer was not leaving her alone. Both times I spent the day with her. This time her desire, however, was that we didn't stay too long. My son and I made a ritual of having dinner with Nanny I think he equated it to going out to dinner. She would watch him, smile and then turn inward to the distance.

Looking back I see this was her way of preparing us. She knew we had to get use to her not being around.

She couldn't believe it happened again. Back in the hospital, she said,

"You could not have paid me for this one."

Perhaps, I was not specific enough.

"I asked God to let me get insurance perhaps I should have asked to stay around long enough to make sure you guys would get the money."

Her eyes glared in disbelief.

Dense fog is the best description I can give of what I have experienced. Kinda' reminds me of an early morning foggy drive in Los Angeles California. Very dense fog unable to see the car one car length in front of me, turning on the headlights makes it worse. My only comfort or confidence is I know where I am going. If I continue slowly and consistently I will get to my destination and eventually the early morning fog will burn away.

I cry and try to remember my childhood. They say remember the good times. I know I had a good childhood, however my ability to remember the joys are missing from my mental database. Constantly, I recount

"Is there something else I could have done?

Did I give up?

Would she still be here if I had not said she did not have to fight for us?

"I am very tired," she whispered.

I knew she did not desire to be dependent on others she often said,

"Confined to a bed is not living."

Lonely, no one really calls to check on me. It is like I am plagued with death and no one wants to be around me. I use to spray "V" repellent—Vulnerability repellant, like Raid bug spray. Now, I long for the opportunity to reveal the inner emptiness of not having my rock, my mother her courage. At one point she said,

"Maybe I should not have come to Las Vegas."

"Maybe I should have stayed in Los Angeles. Baby, you have got to take care of yourself. Mama is not going to be here always."

There is insensitivity to my pain, hurt and lingering weighty discomfort. I have yet to grieve. At least I feel I have not gotten it out. I am told everyone grieves differently.

What does that mean?

Late at night I sit in the room where she took her last breath... and weep.

Am I weeping because my mother is not here?

Am I weeping because I no longer have my savior?

Am I weeping because I have no money and no mother with a 4 year old child and everyone trying to tell me what I should do in this hour of loneliness?

Am I weeping because of all of the above and the fear I will fail without her here?

Recounting the events of my mothers death start like an auto DVD, you know the ones that say "if you do not push play this digital recording will automatically restart."

All I know is the subject matter of grief, accepting the

passing of a significant love one in your life and the preparation of death is not an easy subject. On June, 29, 2009 my mother departed this life at 3:10 am PST.

The return of a five year stretch free of breast cancer that spread to her lungs and two years of treatment only to learn the cancer spread to her brain, spine and bones;

My sister and I received a call she was hospitalized with pneumonia, possibly cancer too. Without question my sister and I took the next flight out to California. I have a strong belief in God! His timing! His healing! His strength! His Divine Purpose in everything in our lives. But she was only 65 years young with a whole lot of life yet to live! *I am sure others say the same about their love ones.* As you can see her passing was 2 days after the announcement of Michael Jacksons and Farah Fawcett's death.

We turned all the TVs off in my house because I did not want my mother to hear the news for fear it could change what I was not ready to accept; the inevitable call to exit this life and cross over to the next. Quite candidly, five months later I think the grief weighs heavier today than when she left.

Often it feels like a wet 2x4 resting comfortably in my heart. I know I did all I could. Everyone gives accolades for how my sister and I took care of my mother as if there was another choice. I do not know that as a professed Christian I or many like me truly prepare for the weight of this experience: Spiritually, Physically or Financially.

Challenged with persistent thoughts of,

Did I give up?

Did I let go too soon?

Meaning my faith…She didn't want to suffer and neither did we want to see her suffer. My mother is out of her pain or the pain of illness and disappointment in this life! She did all she could to prepare my sister and me for her departure! This knowledge does not negate that she is not here! It is quite difficult remembering her smile, her voice, her laughter, her wisdom, her encouragement, just her presence!

My last visual is filled with anguish seeing her suffer and then a cold corpse lying in a casket lowered into the darkness of mother earth.

When she left this life she was home with me, as I said I was taking care of her. The night she left I knew she was leaving us—I remember going in her room, her eyes were open. I turned her music on and touched her head it was scorching hot! I checked her vitals everything was off the Richter scale.

Putting cold towels and icepacks on her forehead, under her arms, and her back I begin to pray and sing…I then told my mother,

"It was o.k. we would be o.k. and that everything was taken care of."

An hour or so later she was gone!

Now my sorrow takes me to thoughts of I would rather have her here and me taking care of her than not have her presence around. I realize that sounds very selfish, but grief is selfish isn't it? Adding to the discomfort and sorrow are the financial challenges. I listen to Janet Jackson answer questions like: How are you dealing with your brother's unexpected death? She replies she's been able to keep busy. A new album, and completed a movie, I listen to those by the side of Farrah Fawcett...pretty much saying the same. Busy is not working for me, I still have flashes that send me into a tail spin; and financial challenges on top of the emotional challenges are not a pretty picture.

I remember thinking about all the fuss over the money being spent on the memorial services for Michael Jackson, I felt like calling the news station and saying if you do not know what to do...

"We need some help and I promise you it is needed."

I say this not to take anything away from the tragedy and loss of Michael, Farrah or anyone else.

Two saving graces: my son, who looks up at me and says,

"I really miss Nanny!"

He will pray,

"I know it has been tough for all of us, and she is in heaven, but we need your help!"

He is only 4.

The second is my belief in God and the strong words of convictions spoken by my mother, *"...there are no mistakes in God!"*

I guess that's 3 saving graces, in honoring the life and memory of my mother by carrying the mantle of her dream to make a difference in the world by making a difference in the lives of those she came in contact with. Am I able to see her dream in my dreams? In this moment of reflection I stop holding my breath.

Ah, I take a Deep breath and breathe...I inhale Ssssssssssssssssssssssssssss!

"You are not the only one facing challenges," I tell myself.

You are not the only person that has witnessed their mother die prematurely, you are not the only person who feels alone or lonely you will get through this.

Bursting out in tears with a deep inner whaling, I do not want my son to hear me weeping.

I look in the mirror at my sobbing red eyes, splash some cold water on my face and say,

Breatheeeeee ....

Exhale....AaaaaaaaaaahhhhhhHhhhhhhhh

I let it out and make every attempt to let it go… It is in an instance, a moment a fresh breeze passes my face and the slight whisper of my mothers' voice….

"It is already alright, now get yourself together, you have a child to raise and things to do, pull it together now before you end up in the grave with me!"

I smile, if you knew my mother, you know she always pulled a reality check that would snap you back into the business at hand.

I desire to have night dreams like others say they have of my mother in their sleep. Even remember more of my childhood. I can not seem to remember much right now. I know I had a good one. Details are faint and sketchy. I look at pictures and I remember moments or occasions: birthdays, Valentines, Thanksgiving, Christmas and of course Mother's Day which I am sure will be tough too. The details are faint. Both of my parents made birthdays special and on Valentines we always shared "Love-U's." Mother's Day and Father's Day were special. We always got together as a family on Thanksgiving and Christmas, but the details… Maybe as I let go of the present discomfort more of the joys and details of my history with my father and mother will surface to the forefront of my mind.

Bottom line is through it all I have surprisingly not given into the emotional, physical and financial pressures and sought refuge and relief by running into the arms of a "Mr., binging on a shopping spree, or making irrational financial decisions," nor the disappointment in those whom I thought would be here for me who have not been here.

I'm competing in the Olympics. My opponent is me. I am ok with time to myself. God has sustained me. I have experienced for myself an assurance and victory that can only be received after being tried and tested. The anguish of accepting how God chooses the outcome of a life crisis has walked me through a living experience of *"Lord your Kingdom Come and your will be done in my earth as it is in heaven."* I have learned and I am learning the meaning of surrender. Matthew 6:10 releases a slight breeze of relief and I do mean slight. *It is enough to invigorate the fragrance of hope and faith!*

I breathe *Inhale…SSsssssssss…ExhaleAAaaHHhhh…*

Not sure how it is ALL going to come together, but for sure I know this. It IS ALL Right!

Not This Time

ORCHESTRATE

∞

"And we know that All things work together for good to them that love God and to them that who are the called according to purpose."

Romans 8:28

"A man or woman gift, talent will make room (a path to prosper) and brings him/her before great men or women."

Proverbs 18:16

∞

Not This Time

∞

I am weak but Lord you are Strong! There is no way I could have orchestrated this moment. Revelation is poured into my heart. I cannot type fast enough. There is no way I could have orchestrated, synchronized or arranged any of what is happening.

Exhaustion, illness and a great deal of concern, missing my mother and my father has been extreme—almost staggering. I push to my commitments and at every spark of energy I hurry to accomplish a task before my fizzle goes flat, like an open container of soda that has been sitting on a kitchen counter for an hour. It is painfully apparent that I have been nowhere near my best lately. My attention is short and scattered to say the least and the battle of maintaining my mind, soul and peace has been unreal.

Each attempt in the direction of overcoming grief, financial upset, physical exhaustion and loneliness has been gnawed at by little critters of silent fear attempting to destroy my very foundation with hallucinations of failure, homelessness, sickness, and death.

Sometimes I cannot find the words to pray. All I can say is…..

Jesus!

Help me God!

I guess I've uttered these words so much, my child is now saying,

Help my mother God; she needs your help in his nightly prayers.

He prays *Lord we are grateful, heal my mother God...*

Then he will put his hand on my head and say,

"HEAL her God!"

"HELP her GOD!"

"WE NEED YOU GOD!"...then he says mama...

How did I pray?

Was it okay?

In those moments I have to smile and laugh...

Yes son, your prayer was just fine.

He reaches over and kisses me on the right cheek, the left cheek, my forehead, my chin and both eyes with

"I love you mama!"

One of the cornerstones of my life is I *Believe*. Before marketing experts decided to use it for Macy's and Cirque du Soleil picked a show and named it "Believe."

God created man in His image and likeness and said *Believe*.

A child is born into this world with no fear! Over time he/she is taught to Fear, doubt is inoculated into the fibers of our veins and imagination is stifled with controls and boundaries not intended by God. Life orchestrates events to rebuild and reconstruct our no fear attitude.

∞

Orchestrate: to compose or arrange (music) for an orchestra: to provide with orchestration: to arrange or combine so as to achieve a desired or maximum effect.

Merriam Webster Dictionary

∞

The quandary persists; the fight is not over, but the battle is won. I am not sure how but reassurance of Zechariah is forced to the front of my memory.

∞

Zechariah 4:6-7; 11 – 14

Verse 6   Then he answered and spoke into me saying, this is the word of the Lord unto Zerubbabel *(sown in Babylon – Gate of God)* saying NOT BY MIGHT *(Shear will)* Not by POWER *(Shear WILL POWER)* but by my SPIRIT *(HIS will & Power Anointing)* says the LORD.

Verse 7 Oh great mountain *(difficulty, persistent nagging challenge and or problem that will not go away)* the same thing again! Before Zerubabel *(sown before the gate of God but still in captivity, imprisonment or custody of a situation that will not give you relief)*

Verse 11 Then answered I, and said unto him, What are these two olive trees upon the right side of the candlestick and upon the left side thereof?

Verse 12 And I answered again, and said unto him, what be the two olive branches which through the two golden pipes empty the golden oil out of themselves?

Verse 13 And he answered me and said, Know thou not what these be? And I said No, my Lord.

Verse 14 The said he, these are the two anointed ones, that stand by the Lord of the whole earth.

∞

In my personal prayer time God gave me revelation on how this scripture represents this part of my journey. My spirit echoes the following words: "You, *the mountain of persistent defeat and fear* shall become a plain, *Flat, simple, basic, unadorned, pure, clear and evident* and He shall bring forth the headstone; *CHRIST-The Savior shall be revealed in the face of my mountain,* with it shouting *declarations and proof of* Grace, *super natural power* Grace, *Super Natural power* unto it. *The persistent, nagging thoughts of defeat and fear will disappear and become* Not just an understanding of the word of God but the miracle power evidence of true transformation.

I am reminded of two anointed men, one that stands by the Lord of the whole earth: *Joshua and Zerubable. Joshua represents the Savoir and Zerubable means that which is sown before the Gate of God! Another way of saying this is my worship and praise given at the feet of God* will produce the Golden oil *or Grace, Grace of God! A double dose of the supernatural power of God!*

Paul confirms this revelation, *for I have come to realize that the sufferings (discomforts, disappointments, frustrations, and persistent naggings) of this present time (experiences) are not worthy to be compared with the glory (magnificence, splendor, beauty, grandeur, brilliance) which shall be revealed in us (transformation /purpose).*

Romans 8:16

∞

Some problems and difficult decisions remind us that we need help from a source outside of self. Some problems and complexities are for us to recognize the growth in self through the Spirit. Challenge, unidentified emotions and uncertain outcomes present themselves in our lives so that we have an opportunity to experience our authentic self in the presence of the supernatural power and hand of God. We have a tendency to think it was our mere discipline, wit or intellect when expected results turn up without experiencing the lesson of surrender or find relief with no empowerment encounter in God. Cycles of ineffective behavior become hidden like blind spots and the past will swallow up your dreams and visions into the abyss of endless defeat when a solid testimony of *If it had not been for the Grace of God* is not birthed and nurtured.

Have you ever heard someone talk about what you should do and how you should choose and live your life and they themselves are in a shambles. Or do not use their advice or take the medicine they recommend you ingest?

It's funny because my Pastor often says,

"Stop saying you didn't ask for this, yes you did when you said whatever you want me to do Lord I will do it, you can use me Lord, where ever you tell me to go I will go, whatever you tell me to do Lord I will do it..."

Now when we get to that verse in songs I stop singing...

Not that I will not do it, just do not want anymore tests than I have to have, because of my insistence in following a good sounding melody.

Yeah! Right, like I can control the process of Gods magnificence in my life.

I have some shocking news,

There is no short-cut, 7-Steps, turn-a-round, click your heals 3 times and say I wish I was home, I wish I was home like Dorothy in the Wizard of Oz, and it will be better. Nope! Doesn't work quite like that!

Our life is orchestrated to bring about a sweet song and melody of worship and praise to the Lord of the universe. It is only stubbornness, resistance, and ignorance that throw in an off note sending out the sound for test intensity. We all have to go through the same thing Jesus Christ did at Gethsemane the crossroad of decisions! We all must die to our own wishes so that our desires can be infused with divine purpose. See the hard fact and truth is no matter what! We have choices and not choosing is choice. Not acting or moving in the direction that your inner guide is directing you to go is choice. Refusing to go through life by sedating self with Mr's, or Sister's, Shopping sprees, ignoring the warning signs, pretending like you are an innocent bystander in this journey, eating binges, drug binges, religious binges, success binges, failure binges, whatever your choice of sedation, is a choice.

My God, *"I do not want to help everybody else and cannot help myself."*

Choosing to sedate does not mean life will not continue to knock on your door and ask for your participation. The only real secret is to let life in! Embrace her! In embracing I have learned you can let go and live. The saying, live, love and laugh can become a real magnet in your day to day experiences.

As I inhale the fear I have learned to exhale my faith. Look in the mirror and say,

Not This Time! Will I repeat what does not work, living in insanity and abnormality calling it normal?

Not this time! Will I let fear walk me down a corridor with flashing red lights with my eyes wide shut refusing to believe them the first time?

Not this time! Will I compromise the innate power given to me by God all mighty when he created me in His image and after His likeness; I am just like HIM;

Not this time! Will I run from myself into the hands of another who has not accepted himself to misuse the softness of my heart and the strength of my character?

Not this time! Will I doubt that the intentions of my Savoir is to ensure that my later days will be better than my former days, and I run from the discomfort of discipline and bringing my mind, soul and will under the authority and Lordship of my GOD, a power that resides in my inner knower that cannot be exchanged for money or its likes.

Not This Time! Will being by myself be mistaken as being alone? I have me in wholeness and peace, the kind of peace that rests on and in my heart even when I am in a room of noise and confusion.

Not This Time! Will I hold onto limits, lack, hurts, disbelief, doubt anxiety and plain old FEAR? I exercise my freedom to live in extreme possibility and Believe that ALL things are Possible with GRACE! GRACE!?

Not This Time! Will I sacrifice my Dream of a world much different than the world I lived in yesterday, not yet experienced neither revealed to common man nor woman; A Dream that my child, my promise, my son of laughter, the one that was not suppose to be can live, touch and experience what his Nanny saw in the far distance. A world full of unstoppable results fueled with imagination, visions and hopes! A world where he, me and we deem as possible that ALL things are not only possible but probable with your Hope & FAITH! I stand on the foundation of NOT THIS TIME!

Confidently judging my world on gratefulness, thankfulness and trust in the infinite power and resources of my Creator the Master of Everything, MY GOD! That has not only declared me as victorious but empowered me with a gift, a story of triumph and sanctioned me with room to share my divine purpose of it was *You Again?...but Not This Time!*

What stirs in my Spirit is a poise that could not have been synchronized by mere words on a page— Intellectual and Spiritual jargon. The freshness of my journey had to be fully clinched in the imprisonment of my mind and my physical world. In the presence of death, defeat and denial Not This Time had to live! The words must leap off the pages with convictions and truth, not just facts, but a reality experience that would touch your soul, mind, and your will.

Do I want to lie close to a warm body hugging me saying it will be all right?

Yes!

Do I want to kick my feet up and say enough is enough I am tired and this is not working?

Yes!

Do I want to question the legitimacy of miraculous healing and the raising of the dead?

Yes!

Do I want to be careless, loose lipped and straighten all the lies and misunderstandings that have preceded my name "Daughter of Promise, reflection of Wisdom knowledge, understanding and wealth"?

Yes!

Do I want to question will I ever live out MY DREAM?

Yes!

Do I want instant gratification?

Yes!

Do I want to do what I want to do and make things happen the way I think I can?

Yes!

But,

Not by my willpower, I have come this far trusting in the everlasting promise and power of MY GOD!

Not This Time!

Not This Time

THANK YOU

I am eternally grateful for those who have enriched my life particularly within the last six years. You have challenged me to stand and walk out what I believe, for that thank you!

I could not have completed this work without the love and encouragement of my brother and sister Pastor Marc C. & Lady LaShon Hawthorne. You have been more than family but a Spiritual guide.

Toni, Lori, Tim, Yolanda, Aisha, Rosalind, Mom Mary, The Wimbley's and Lisa you will never know how much I appreciate your support, prayers, and love! Thank you!

My son, who has lent me to the world and knew when to leave me alone, Thank you!

Finally, to my Lord and Savior Jesus Christ I am nothing, cannot do anything without you, Thank you!

∞

Not This Time

Additional books by iRiS the Dream Whisperer

For additional information or to purchase products, Dream Shops series or have iRiS at your next event.

Email: MoorePublishingInc@yahoo.com
Website: www.iRiSTalks.com
Or write
iRiS
3635 S. Fort Apache Road Suite 200-429
Las Vegas, NV 89147

Management:
LHM Management Group
11807 Westheimer Road Unit 550-112
Houston, TX 77077
Phone No.: 832-493-3641

Not This Time

Not This Time

www.ingramcontent.com/pod-product-compliance
Lightning Source LLC
Chambersburg PA
CBHW060750180626
46818CB00002B/522